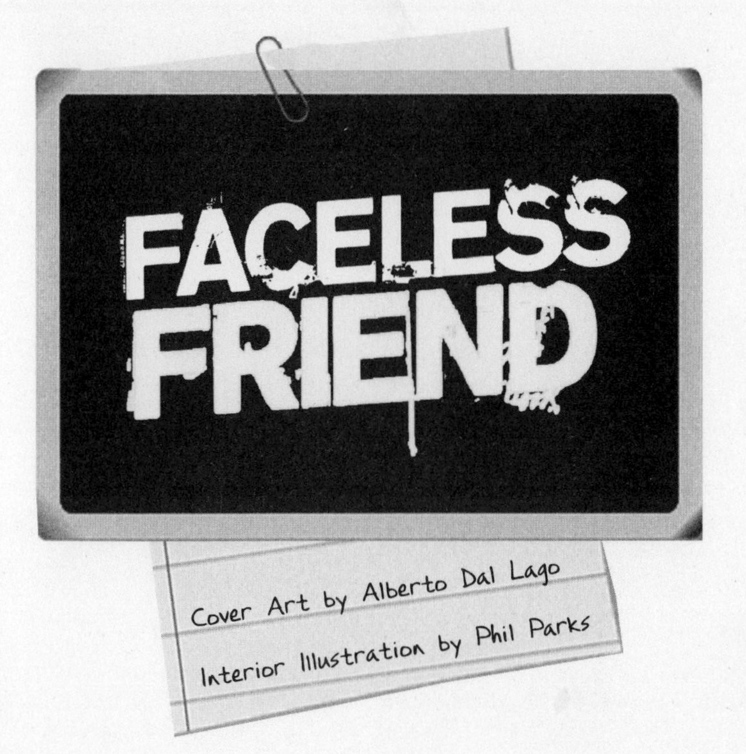

STONE ARCH BO
a capstone imprint

Jason Strange is published by
Stone Arch Books
A Capstone Imprint
151 Good Counsel Drive, P.O. Box 669
Mankato, Minnesota 56002
www.capstonepub.com

Library of Congress Cataloging-in-Publication Data is available on the Library of Congress website.

Summary: When Chase Beckett wakes up one morning, he discovers that no one recognizes him at middle school.

ISBN 978-1-4342-3232-8 (library binding)
ISBN 978-1-4342-3431-5 (pbk.)

Photo credits:
Shutterstock: Nikita Rogul (handcuffs, p. 2); Stephen Mulcahey (police badge, p. 2); B&T Media Group (blank badge, p. 2); Picsfive (coffee stain, pp. 2, 5, 12, 17, 24, 30, 42, 48, 57); Andy Dean Photography (paper, pen, coffee, pp. 2, 66); osov (blank notes, p. 1); Thomas M Perkins (folder with blank paper, pp. 66, 67); M.E. Mulder (black electrical tape, pp. 69, 70, 71)

Art Director/Graphic Designer: Kay Fraser

Printed in the United States of America in Stevens Point, Wisconsin.
032011
006111WZF11

TABLE OF CONTENTS

RAVENS
6:30

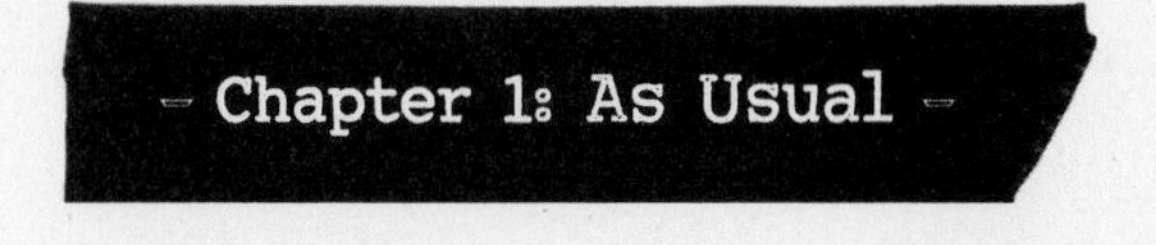

Chapter 1: As Usual

My alarm went off at six thirty that Monday morning, like it always did on Monday mornings. I skipped the shower and headed downstairs.

It was dark. I was the first one up, as usual, and I poured myself a bowl of Sugar Bombs by the light of the open refrigerator. I ate the cereal in front of the TV.

By the time I was done, the sun was nearly up.

The bus would get to the corner in a few minutes. I grabbed my baseball glove from the shelf by the front door, along with the baseball folded inside it, and walked outside.

The bus stop was a block away. The weather was perfect: still nice and crisp that early, but the sun was still low. By that afternoon's game, it would be in the low seventies, I could tell. Perfect weather for my first start of the season, pitching for the Ravens Pass Middle School baseball team.

"Hey," I said when I reached the corner. There was my longtime neighbor and once-friend, Jessica — though I just called her Ick, like most of the other people in eighth grade. She was a year behind me at Ravens Pass Middle School.

Ick was sitting on the curb with a comic book inches from her nose.

I leaned over behind her so my knees knocked her in the back. "How can you read in this light?" I said with a laugh.

She didn't answer. She just inched forward on the curb a little so my knees weren't touching her anymore.

I shrugged and pulled on my mitt, and then tossed my ball straight up. It fell back into my glove with a smack. I loved that sound.

After a couple of tosses, I heard the bus coming toward us down Poppy Street. When I stopped tossing the ball, I realized Ick was staring at me. "What?" I said.

"I was wondering," Ick said. She closed her comic and slipped it into her backpack. Then she stood up. "Is that all you're bringing? A mitt and a baseball?"

"That's very funny," I said. The bus's brakes squeaked loudly and then hissed. The door flew open and I went to get on.

"I wasn't trying to be funny," Ick said.

"You know it's all I bring to school," I said. "I've only ever brought my glove and a ball every day since around fourth grade." I shook my head and climbed aboard.

"How would I know what you've been doing since fourth grade?" she asked, following me onto the bus.

I stopped in the aisle and turned to face her. "Maybe if you'd take your nose out of the comic books for half a minute," I said quickly, "you'd notice things like that."

Ick didn't reply. She just slid into a seat near the front and opened her bag. I guess she was taking out the comic again.

I went to the back of the bus and took my normal spot in the last row and stared out the window. The bus started off again, rolling along Century Avenue next to the river.

Chapter 2: Stood Up

After a quick stop at my locker, I headed over to Benny's locker near the auditorium. He'd been my best friend for years. Since the first day of sixth grade, we'd met at his locker every day before heading to first period.

I leaned against the cold metal locker and watched the clock outside Mr. Drone's office. There were only a couple of minutes until class started.

Benny was late.

I was about to give up. Then the scrawny kid whose locker was next to Benny's rushed over and started working on his lock.

"Hey . . . um," I said. I couldn't remember his name, but he didn't seem to notice.

"What?" he asked. He looked at me nervously. "Do you need something?"

"Have you seen Benny yet today?" I asked. "The guy with this locker."

"Yeah, I know who Benny is," the kid said. "Everyone does. And yes. He was here when I was, a few minutes ago. I just had to run back because I forgot my math homework in my bag."

"Why didn't he wait for me?" I asked. I wasn't exactly asking him. I was just sort of talking to myself — thinking out loud.

"Um, why would he do that?" the scrawny kid said. He grabbed a few pieces of paper and slammed the locker door. Then he ran off down the hall toward the math and science wing.

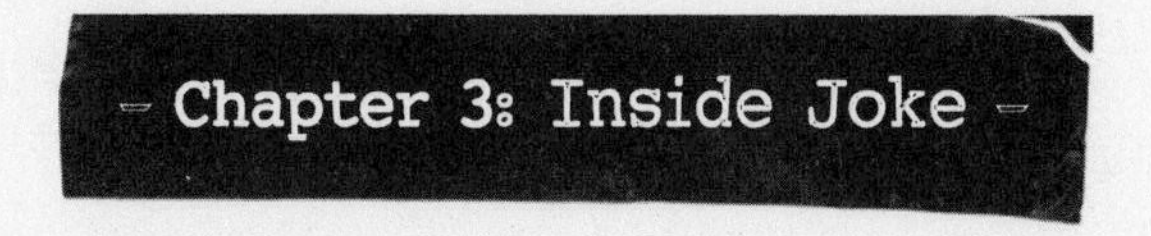

Chapter 3: Inside Joke

My first period class was nearly full by the time I got there.

We don't have assigned seats in Mr. Jackson's class. He thinks it makes class more interesting, or something.

One seat right in the front — right in front of Mr. Jackson's desk — was empty. I slid into the seat, out of breath, and turned around to look for Benny.

He was in the back row, talking to Paul Simpson and Katie Shoo. They were laughing.

We had a few minutes before Mr. Jackson would take attendance. I jogged to the back and sat on the edge of Benny's desk.

"What are you guys laughing about?" I asked, smiling.

The three of them suddenly stopped laughing. They turned to me with blank looks on their faces. "Um," Katie said, "excuse us?"

"Yeah, dude," Paul said. "This is, like, a private conversation."

"Are you serious?" I asked.

Mr. Jackson cleared his throat and tapped his pen on the desk. "Seats, please," he said.

I ran up to the front and sat down, but my stomach was doing flips.

What is with everyone this morning? I thought. It was like I'd woken up in the Twilight Zone.

Mr. Jackson started taking attendance. I sat back and listened for my name. Most people were there.

Mr. Jackson got all the way to Ty Zinn. But he didn't call my name.

"Mr. Jackson," I said, raising my hand. "You didn't say my name."

Mr. Jackson looked at his list and then looked at me. He frowned. "Oh, I'm very sorry," he said, shaking his head. "I didn't know we had a new student in class today. In fact, Principal Drone didn't tell me anything about you."

"A new . . . ," I began. Then I shook my head. "No, I'm Chase Beckett. I've been in this class all year."

"Right," Mr. Jackson said. He adjusted his glasses and looked back at the paper. Then he picked up his red pen. "For now, I'll just put your name down here. Chase Beckman, was it?"

"Beckett," I said. Then I laughed. "What is this? Some kind of joke or something? I've been in this class as long as everyone else. I'm not new to the class, or to the school, or to Ravens Pass."

Someone laughed in the back row. A bunch of people started whispering. I heard a voice say, "Crazy."

I had to agree. Mr. Jackson was acting crazy.

"I'm sure we'll clear it all up," Mr. Jackson said. "Now, if you don't mind, let's get class started."

I shook my head and mumbled, "Go ahead." But I knew I wouldn't be learning anything that morning. There was no way I'd be able to concentrate. Something weird was going on.

Chapter 4: Off the Team?

I stayed quiet until lunch.

In classes, I didn't try telling any teachers my name or chatting with other people in class.

In the hall after second period, I tried saying a quick hello to the baseball team's best hitter, a guy I'd played ball with for years.

He looked at me like I had four heads, then said, "Um, hey."

When lunch finally rolled around, I walked to the cafeteria as quickly as I could and found Benny and Clyde. I'd eaten lunch with them every day since we all joined the team together, back in sixth grade.

"Guys, I am having the strangest day ever," I said as I sat down with my tray of food. I put my glove and ball down on the table.

Benny and Clyde looked at each other, then at me. "Okay, dude," Clyde said. They both laughed.

"I'm serious," I said. I opened my carton of chocolate milk and took a long swig. "For instance, I saw Emmitt in the hall earlier today, and —"

"Hey," Benny said, interrupting me. "I'm sorry, but why do you think we would care?"

"Shut up, Benny," I said. "I'm not in the mood."

Benny shrugged. Then he seemed to notice my glove on the table. "Hey, you play baseball?" he asked.

I rolled my eyes. "Okay, enough goofing around, Benny," I said. "You know I play baseball."

"Riiiiight," Benny said. "That looks like a pitcher's mitt. Do you pitch?"

"I've been pitching since sixth grade," I said. I shook my head. What was wrong with everyone today?

"Well, listen to me, new kid," Benny said. "I am the starting pitcher at Ravens Pass Middle School. I have been for over two years. I'm not going to let some new weird kid take that spot from me. Got it?"

“What?” I asked. I was so shocked I could hardly talk, so it sounded like a whisper, or a gasp for breath.

“Just stay away from the mound,” Benny said. “Better yet, stay away from the field.”

“And stay away from us,” Clyde added. They high-fived and laughed.

I picked up my tray and walked off to find somewhere else to eat . . . alone.

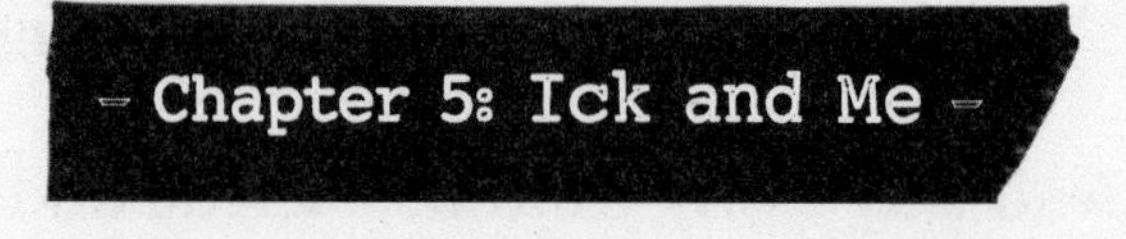

Chapter 5: Ick and Me

The cafeteria was packed, because it was lunchtime for most of the seventh and eighth grade. There wasn't anywhere I could eat alone. There was one table where only one person was sitting. Ick.

I dropped my tray quietly and slid into the plastic chair. The food in front of me didn't look so great, and I had no appetite anyway. I just poked at it with my fork and sipped my chocolate milk.

At the other end of the table, Ick hardly looked up from her comic. But once in a while, she stole a glance at me.

"Hey," she finally said. "Aren't you the weird kid from the bus stop this morning?"

I sighed. "I'm the weird kid?" I said. "You're the one who reads comic books twenty-four hours a day and has like no friends."

Ick squinted at me and nodded slowly. "Yup, you're him," she said. "Can I give you some advice?"

I shrugged and poked at my mashed potatoes and lumpy gravy.

"You're new here. I know that it's hard to be the new kid," she said. "But don't make too many enemies."

"New here?" I repeated. "I'm not —"

"Listen, if you don't want to be friends with me, no problem," Ick said. She chuckled. "It's not like I'm an important person to know at this school. But Benny and Clyde? Stay out of their way and you'll do a lot better, know what I mean? You don't want them as enemies. They're very powerful. They can ruin your life like that." Ick snapped her fingers and I jumped. Then she went back to reading her comic book.

"Hey," I said. "Why does everyone keep calling me a new kid?"

Ick looked up. "Well, you are, right?" she said.

"No!" I replied. I was practically shouting. "Jessica, I'm Chase Beckett. I've known you for more than ten years. We used to have play dates together when we were little kids. Don't you remember me?"

CHIP

"I can't remember even seeing you before," Ick said. "And I certainly don't remember having a date with you. As if I'd go on one with you in the first place. I don't even know you." She sniffed, and then started to push her chair back, like she was afraid of me or something.

"Not a date," I said. "A play date. We were, like, toddlers. Babies!"

"Well, I guess I forgot, then," Ick said. I think she was being sarcastic. "I forgot you completely."

"You and everyone else today, it seems," I said. My shoulders sagged.

Ick put a hand on her bag like she was thinking about getting up.

"Go ahead and leave," I said. "I'm destined to be alone anyway."

"Wait a minute, Chase," Ick said. She leaned forward in her chair. "Are you saying you woke up this morning and no one could remember who you are?"

"That's right," I said.

Ick's face lit up with a smile and she dug around in her backpack for a second. Her little hands came out gripping a rolled-up comic book. Then she jumped up from her chair, ran around the table, and dove into the chair next to me.

"Look at this," she said, leaning right up to me.

"Um," I said, "what is it?"

"A comic," Ick said. "Boy, you are weird."

"I know it's a comic," I said. "I mean, why should I care about some silly comic book?"

"Look here," she said. She flipped through the pages to the middle. "This guy woke up normal and everything, but then when he got to school . . ."

She pointed to a drawing of the main character sitting on a curb in front of his school, with his head in his hands and his elbows on his knees.

The thought bubble over his head said, *Why doesn't anyone remember me?*

"It's just like me," I said quietly. "What are the chances of that? This is totally bizarre."

"I know," Ick said. "It's pretty creepy. That this is happening to you, I mean."

I flipped to the back of the comic and scanned the pictures and words. "So?" I said. "What happens to this guy?"

Ick grabbed the comic from me and rolled it up. "I don't know," she said. "The next issue isn't out until next week."

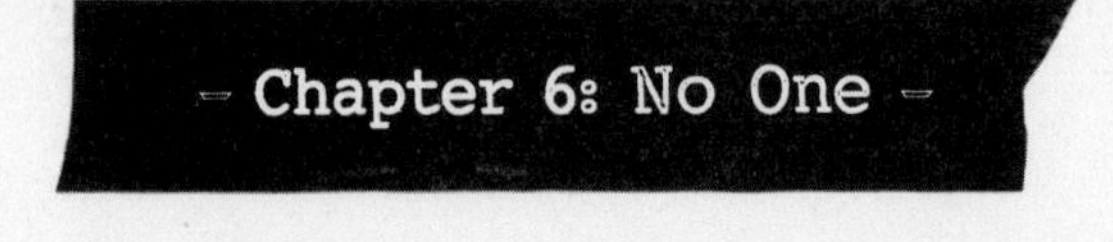

Chapter 6: No One

"Arg!" I said. I got up and grabbed my tray. "This is pointless."

I dumped my food into the trash and put my tray on the bus table. Then I stormed through the double doors and into the halls.

"Where are you going?" Ick called behind me. She had followed me out of the cafeteria and was walking quickly to catch up.

"Who cares?" I said. "I don't exist. I'm no one now."

TODA
HEAL

"Oh, don't be so dramatic," Ick said. She'd caught up and was walking next to me. I was impressed, actually. She was really fast.

I remembered back in third grade, when Ick was in second grade, we used to have races around the baseball diamond at the park. Ick used to win.

"Listen," she went on. "I've seen movies like this — TV episodes, comics, books. It happens all the time. I guess I never thought it could happen for real."

"So?" I said. We got to the front doors of the school and I stopped.

"So, I can figure out how to fix this," Ick said. "Like, um . . ."

She nibbled her fingernail for a second. "Maybe it's amnesia," she said, her eyes wide.

I shook my head. "If it was amnesia," I said, "I would have forgotten everyone else. They'd still remember me."

"Oh, right," she said. "Maybe everyone else has amnesia!"

I glared at her. "I doubt it, Ick," I said.

Ick shrugged. "Okay, so it's not amnesia," she said.

She went back to nibbling her fingernail. Suddenly, with her fingertip between her lips, her eyes got wide and her face went pale. She stared at me. Her eyes looked a little watery, like she might cry.

"What?" I said. "Why are you staring like that?"

"You're dead," she said in a low voice.

"Oh, come on," I said.

"I'm telling you," Ick said, still in that breathy spooky voice. "You're dead."

She backed up from me and walked all the way around me, like she was looking at a magician's trick and trying to find the strings or mirrors.

"It happens all the time in movies," she said. "You know, like this is just some temporary place for you on your way to the afterlife. Maybe you have to solve a crime or something."

Ick got right in my face and gave me a creepy look. She said in a deep voice, "You must discover the identity of your murderer!" Then she threw her head back and laughed like a villain.

"This is ridiculous," I said. "And I still say you're the weird one."

"Fine, maybe it is ridiculous," Ick said. "If you say you're alive, I'll agree . . . for now. But let's try this!" Then she reached out and pinched my arm. Hard.

"Ow!" I said. I pulled my arm away and jumped back. "What was that for?"

"I had to make sure you're not dreaming," she said. "It would be pretty silly to get all upset over a silly dream, right?"

"I give up," I said.

I pushed open the front doors and walked out. The sun was nice and high. I could smell the fresh-cut grass. It made me want to pitch a few innings.

The thought just depressed me, though. In my new life, Benny was the pitcher. And he was a big bully, who wouldn't let me near the team.

"Where are you going?" Ick called after me.

"Home," I said. I was thinking I'd crawl into bed and hope this whole weird situation fixed itself. "No point in staying here."

"But, Chase," Ick said. "What if . . ."

I stopped and turned to face her. "What?" I said.

"Your parents," she said. "What if your parents don't know who you are?"

Chapter 7: Homeless and Hopeless

"Where will I live?" I said. "How will I even survive?"

Ick and I were sitting on the curb in front of the school. My head was in my hands. I probably looked just like the guy from Ick's comic book. I felt totally hopeless. It was the worst day of my life.

"We can fix this," Ick said. She put an arm around me and patted my shoulder. "Seriously."

"You don't have to help me," I said. I turned my head and squinted at her. "You don't owe me anything, you know."

"I know," she said.

"Besides," I said, "I can cut classes. No one knows who I am. I don't even think I'm a student at this school anymore. But you'll get in trouble if you don't get back in there."

"I'll be fine," Ick said. "I know how to make sure I never get in trouble for anything."

I picked up my head and looked across the street at the pizza place. It was Sal's Famous Pizza, my favorite food. Back when we were little, Ick's family and my family used to get together there for pizza almost every Friday night.

"I didn't eat any of my lunch," I said.

"Me either," Ick said. She got up and nodded toward the pizza place. For a second, I thought she'd remembered going there with me. But of course she didn't. "Sal's is really good," she said. "Come on. I'll buy."

I smiled and got up too. Then Ick and I jogged across the street.

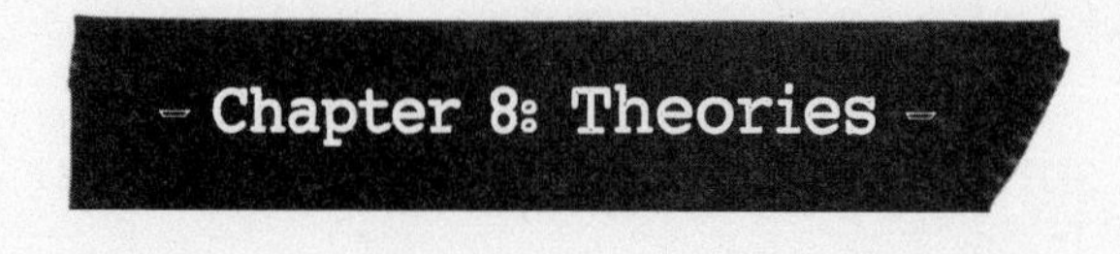

Chapter 8: Theories

At lunch, Ick told me about a bunch of books that this had happened in. She had a few of them in her backpack. She took them out and showed them to me while we ate. There were a couple of other books that she mentioned, but she didn't have those.

"Wow," I said as Ick finished her second slice. "I haven't had lunch with you since third grade, probably. But I see you still love pizza."

"It sure is weird that you know so much about me," she said. "I mean, since I don't remember you at all."

"Sorry," I said. "I'll try to stop creeping you out."

She shrugged. "Listen," she said. She waved her hand over the comics and science-fiction books on the table between us. "I have a few theories about what's going on here."

"So far, we know I'm not dreaming," I said. "And I don't have amnesia."

"And we're assuming for the moment that you're not dead," Ick said.

"Right," I agreed.

"Okay, that leaves a few options," she said. "One: witches."

"Seriously?" I said.

"Sure," Ick said. "Witches exist. I mean, I don't know if they can actually do magic or spells or whatever. But they exist. I've seen them, lots of times."

"Okay," I said. "So, tell me about witches."

Ick opened one of the comics. "In this one, a witch casts a hate spell on a whole town," she said. "Everyone the main character knows suddenly hates him. Obviously, it's not exactly the same. But it's close."

"What else do you have?" I asked, looking at the covers of the books in front of us.

"In this book," Ick said, holding up a thick paperback, "the criminal releases a nerve gas into a city. It makes everyone want to give him their money and possessions."

"Cool," I said. "Maybe if everyone was giving me their money, this wouldn't feel so bad." I thought about it for a second. Then I said, "Actually, it would still feel bad. But at least I'd have a lot of money and stuff, right?"

Ick laughed and held the book across the table. I took the book. On the cover was a man in a suit like they wear when they fix the sewers. His face covered with a hood and mesh mask.

"Who's this guy?" I asked.

"That's the hero," Ick said. "He was in that outfit when the gas was released, so he was spared. He has to find the cure."

"Lucky," I said. I put the book down.

"So have you worn a special suit like that lately?" Ick asked.

"Of course not," I said. "Why?"

"Well, if someone released a forgetting gas," she said, "and if you were wearing that suit, you might have been accidentally spared. It was a long shot, but we have to check every angle."

"What about the witch angle?" I asked.

"Do you have any enemies?" she asked.

I shrugged. "Maybe some of the players on the East Riverton Eagles," I said. "They've lost against me twice this season, both in no-hitters." I leaned back and smiled, proud of my record.

"I don't think any of them could have done this," Ick said, rolling her eyes.

"Why not?" I said. "It made them pretty mad, especially the second time."

"I bet it did," she said. "But it's a very complicated spell, and the players on that team are not very bright."

"How do you know?" I asked.

"I've seen their test scores," she said.

"How did you see their test scores?" I asked.

Ick smiled. "I guess there are a few things you don't know about me after all," she said. "Like how well I can get around in computer systems."

"Sneaky," I said.

"Okay, so no witches, and you didn't wear a gas mask lately," Ick said. "That leaves one last theory."

"What?" I asked.

"It's not good," Ick told me.

She held up a comic book. On the cover was a big, gray building. It loomed over a vast wasteland, and in its shadow was a single man. He cowered before the building, scared for his life.

"Here we go," she said. "A government conspiracy."

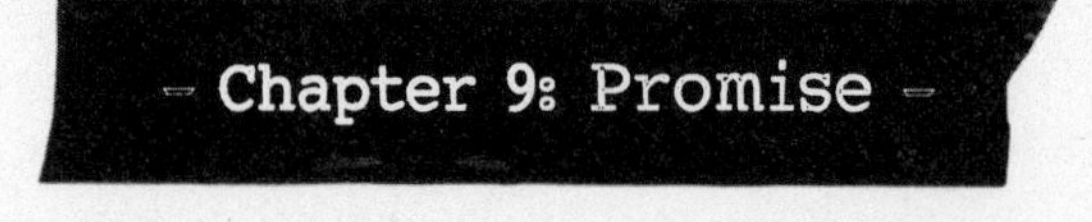

Chapter 9: Promise

"The question is," Ick said as we left Sal's, "why you?"

"You got me," I said. "This is all getting weirder by the moment."

"I better get back to school," Ick said. She glanced at her watch. "I already missed seventh period. One detention is enough."

"What am I going to do?" I said. I grabbed her wrist so she wouldn't walk off. She glared at my hand.

"Sorry," I said. I let go.

"It's okay," she said. "I'll help you. But for now I have to get back."

"I understand," I said. But I wished Ick would stay and help me.

"I'll be back," she said. "Meet me right here after school is out. We can go over to my house and do some research."

"About what?" I asked.

"The government conspiracy," Ick said. "We'll use my computers. I can get into any system in the world. If there's information about you in some government system, I'll find it. This will be over in no time. I promise."

"Okay," I said. "Thanks."

Ick smiled and turned to walk off.

She only got about one step before I called out after her.

"I'm sorry," I said.

She stopped and turned toward me. "Sorry?" she repeated, a confused look on her face. "Sorry for what?"

I shrugged. "I haven't always been so nice to you," I said. "Yeah, we used to be friends, back in grade school. But for a while now, we've been anything but friends."

"What do you mean?" Ick asked. She walked closer to me. "What did you do that wasn't nice?"

I chewed my cheek. "You want an example?" I said.

Ick nodded. "Yeah," she said. "I mean, it's not like I remember any of it."

"Well, your name, for one thing," I said. "It was Benny and me who started calling you Ick instead of Jessica."

"Oh," she said. She looked at her feet. "Well, that wasn't very nice."

"I know," I said. "I've always felt bad about it. I never meant for it to become a big thing. But then, it just stuck. All the other guys thought it was so funny. They thought I was so funny. It got away from me."

"What else?" Ick asked.

There was so much. I took a deep breath and started talking.

There was the time we'd put a tack on her seat on the bus.

There was the rumor we spread last year about how she still wet the bed.

SAL'S

There was the time Benny stole a bunch of her comic books and blacked out all the words with a marker.

I'd laughed the whole time he was doing it, even though I also wanted to stop him. I'd never told her who'd done it, even though I knew, and even though she'd cried on the bus the whole ride home.

When I was done, Ick stared at me for a long time. I thought she might cry.

Instead she said, "And now you're sorry?"

I nodded. "So sorry," I said. "I really am. I wish I'd never done those things. I wish you and I were still friends."

She was quiet for a long time. Then she said, "Well, we are now, right?"

"Right," I said.

"And when this is all over," she said, "and everyone knows who you are again, when you're popular again, when Benny and Clyde want to hang out with again, we'll still be friends. Right?"

"Always," I said. "You've already proven you're a great friend, and you didn't even know who I was. I will never turn my back on you again."

"Promise," she said.

"I promise," I said. I put out my pinky for a pinky swear, and she took it with hers. We hadn't done that in years.

"Okay then," she said. She took a step back and smiled at me. Then she snapped her fingers.

- Chapter 10: Friends Forever -

For an instant, the world around me flooded with light. My head shook with pain, like the worst headache ever. Then everything went dark.

A moment later I came to, sitting on the sidewalk in front of Sal's Famous Pizza.

Ick was standing over me with her hands on her hips. She was staring down at me. I rubbed my eyes.

With the sun behind her, and the strap from her shoulder bag across her chest, Ick looked like some kind of magical warrior.

"Are you okay?" she asked. I couldn't see her face, but I thought she was smiling.

I shook my head to clear it. "I think so," I said. "What happened?"

"Don't worry about it," she said. She put out her hand to help me up, and I took it. "Now we better get back to school. I have a feeling your afternoon teachers will know who you are, and they'll be expecting you."

"You . . . ," I said, staring at her dumbly.

"Friends, right?" she said. Her smirk might have seemed friendly a moment ago, but now it sent a shiver across my shoulders.

"Friends," I said. "Forever." What choice did I have?

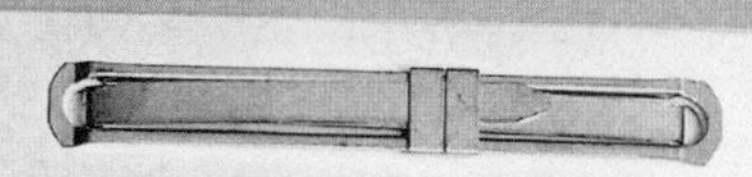

THE FORGOTTEN KID CASE

Case number: 264563

Date reported: March 29

Crime scene: Ravens Pass Middle School

Local police: None

Victim: Chase Beckett, age 14

Civilian witnesses: Staff and student body of Ravens Pass Middle School

Disturbance: Enforced unrecognition spell cast on the victim.

Suspect information: Jessica "Ick" Cavendish, age 14

CASE NOTES:

THE VICTIM CALLED ME HIMSELF, LOOKING FOR HELP. HE DIDN'T WANT THE POLICE INVOLVED, AND I UNDERSTOOD. IT COULD BE EMBARRASSING, IF THIS STORY GOT OUT.

SO IT SEEMS THE GIRL CAST A SPELL ON HIM. NOT A LOVE SPELL. A REVENGE SPELL OF ENFORCED UNRECOGNITION. PRETTY HIGH-LEVEL STUFF, REALLY, FOR A FOURTEEN-YEAR-OLD. AT FIRST, I WANTED TO HAND HER OVER TO AUTHORITIES WHO COULD DEAL WITH HER. BUT ONCE THE BOY TOLD ME THE WHOLE STORY, I HAD TO THINK. FOR ONCE, I FELT THE VICTIM DESERVED WHAT WAS COMING TO HIM.

TWO RIGHTS DON'T MAKE A WRONG, IT'S TRUE. SO I DID CONTACT THE AUTHORITIES—NOT THE POLICE, THE AUTHORITIES WHO DEAL WITH THIS KIND OF THING. BUT I GAVE THE BOY A WARNING, TOO. AFTER ALL, YOU NEVER KNOW WHO KNOWS HOW TO CAST A REVENGE SPELL. I DON'T THINK HE'LL MAKE THAT MISTAKE AGAIN.

DEAR READER,

THEY ASKED ME TO WRITE ABOUT MYSELF. THE FIRST THING YOU NEED TO KNOW IS THAT JASON STRANGE IS NOT MY REAL NAME. IT'S A NAME I'VE TAKEN TO HIDE MY TRUE IDENTITY AND PROTECT THE PEOPLE I CARE ABOUT. YOU WOULDN'T BELIEVE THE THINGS I'VE SEEN, WHAT I'VE WITNESSED. IF PEOPLE KNEW I WAS TELLING THESE STORIES, SHARING THEM WITH THE WORLD, THEY'D TRY TO GET ME TO STOP. BUT THESE STORIES NEED TO BE TOLD, AND I'M THE ONLY ONE WHO CAN TELL THEM.

I CAN'T TELL YOU MANY DETAILS ABOUT MY LIFE. I CAN TELL YOU I WAS BORN IN A SMALL TOWN AND LIVE IN ONE STILL. I CAN TELL YOU I WAS A POLICE DETECTIVE HERE FOR TWENTY-FIVE YEARS BEFORE I RETIRED. I CAN TELL YOU I'M STILL OUT THERE EVERY DAY AND THAT CRAZY THINGS ARE STILL HAPPENING.

I'LL LEAVE YOU WITH ONE QUESTION—IS ANY OF THIS TRUE?

JASON STRANGE

RAVENS PASS

Glossary

afterlife (AF-tur-life)—what happens after death

amnesia (am-NEE-zhuh)—a partial or total loss of memory that can be temporary or permanent

assigned (uh-SINED)—given or supposed to be used each time

auditorium (aw-di-TOR-ee-uhm)—a large room where people gather for meetings, plays, concerts, or other events

concentrate (KON-suhn-trate)—focus thoughts and attention on something

conspiracy (kuhn-SPIHR-uh-see)—a secret plan

dramatic (druh-MAT-ik)—making a fuss

identity (eye-DEN-ti-tee)—who you are

normal (NOR-muhl)—usual or regular

spared (SPAIRD)—not hurt; left alone

temporary (TEM-puh-rer-ee)—lasting for a short time

theory (THIHR-ee)—ideas or opinions

DISCUSSION QUESTIONS

1. Ick cast a spell to make everyone forget Chase. Why did she do this?

2. Sometimes, two people are friends when they're young, but then they grow apart. Why does this happen? What can two friends do to make sure that this doesn't happen?

3. What was the creepiest part of this book? Explain your answer.

WRITING PROMPTS

1. Chase loves baseball, and Ick loves comic books. What's your favorite hobby? Write about it.

2. This is a horror story. Write your own horror story.

3. If everyone forgot you, what would you do? Write about it!

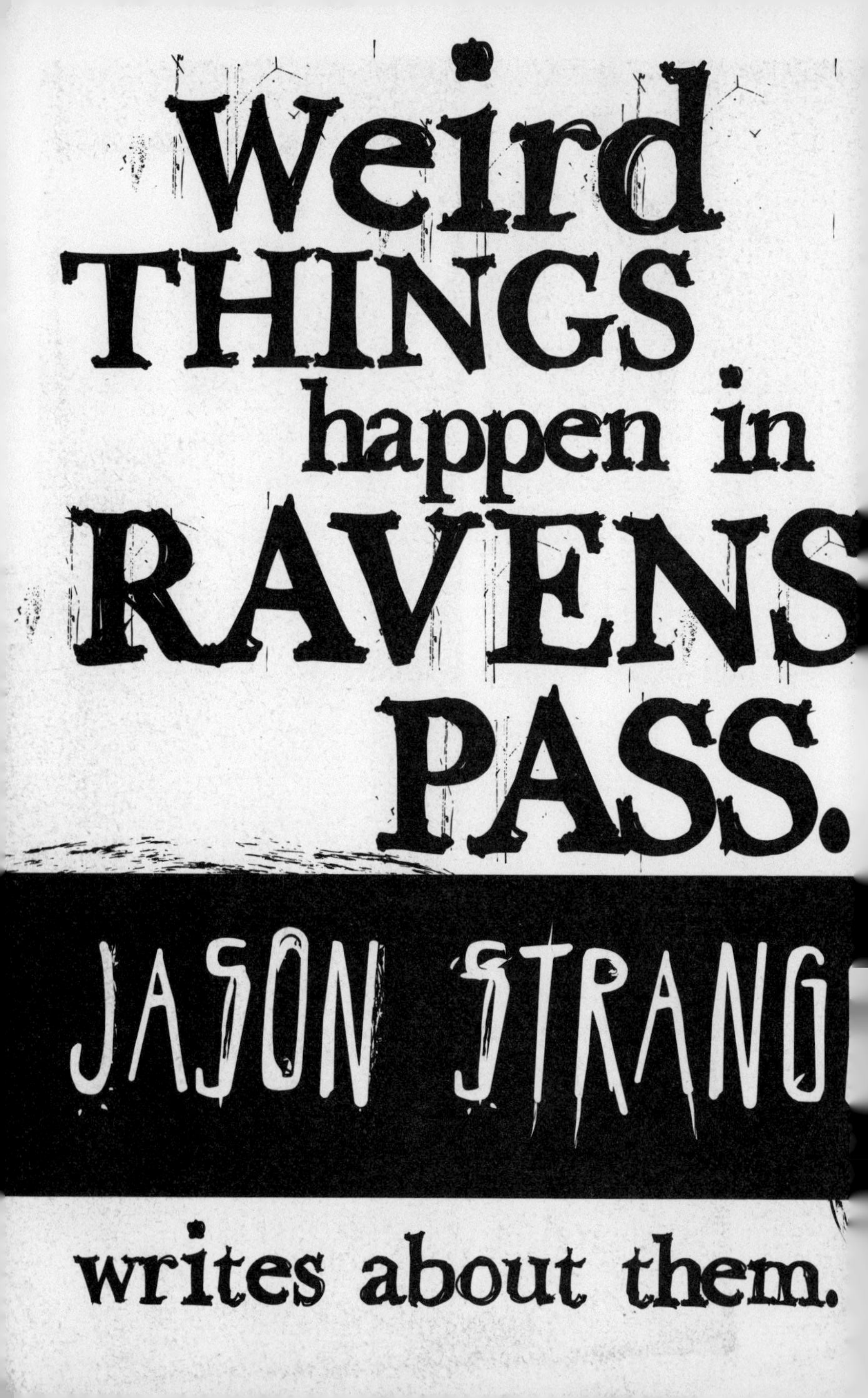
Weird THINGS happen in RAVENS PASS.
JASON STRANG
writes about them.

JASON STRANGE
Text 4 REVENGE
JASON STRANGE
FULL MOON HORROR
JASON STRANGE
BASEMENT OF THE UNDEAD